Buster and the Baby

written by
Amy Hest

illustrated by
Polly Dunbar

WALKER BOOKS
AND SUBSIDIARIES

LONDON · BOSTON · SYDNEY · AUCKLAND

THUMP,
THUMP,
THUMP.

In the little
red house,

a dog
ducks under
the table.

His name is
Buster and
under the table
is a good place
to hide.

(Maybe.)

He waits. And watches. And waits some more.

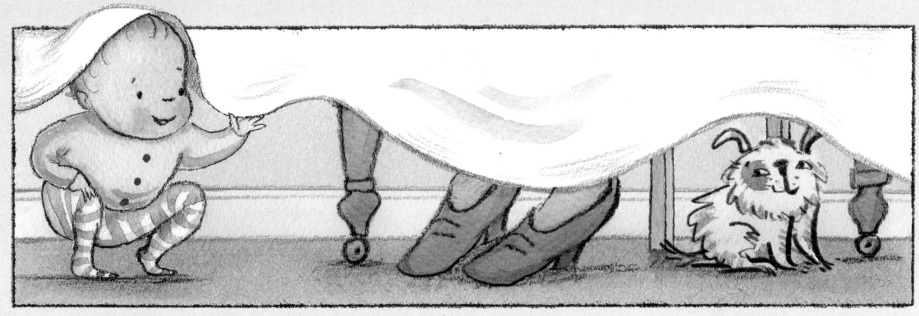

THUMP, goes his heart.

THUMP, *THUMP*, *THUMP!*

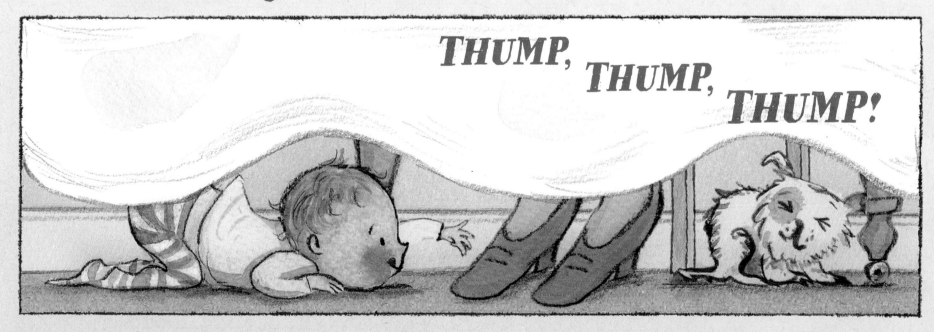

Then...

Out of the shadows she comes.

Squealing and whirling
and bumping
his nose!

He wriggles
behind
the chair.

Behind
the blue chair
is a good place
to hide.

(Maybe.)

He waits. And watches. And waits some more.

THUMP, goes his heart.

THUMP,
THUMP,
THUMP!

Then...

Out of the shadows she comes.

Squealing and whirling
and chasing
his tail!

He leaps
round
the back
of big bear.

Round
the back of big bear
is a good place
to hide.
     (Maybe.)

He waits. And watches. And waits some more.

THUMP, goes his heart.

Then...

Out of the shadows she comes.

Squealing and whirling
and hurling peas!
Ping go the peas.

Ping,

ping,

ping!

Buster
and the baby
go,

go,

But night
always follows day,
and when night comes,
the baby is tucked up
once and for all
in her silvery bed,
in her silvery room.

She hides.

Under
her blanket
is a good place
to hide.

She waits. And watches. And waits some more.

THUMP! goes her heart...

THUMP,
THUMP,
THUMP!

Then...

CHAAA!

Out of the shadows he comes.

Wagging and skidding
across the room!

Up, up, up
on the bed ...

licking her nose,
licking her ears –
lick, lick,
**lickety-
lick!**

Soon,
everyone is yawning.

Thump, go their hearts,
thump, thump, thump.

All through

the night.

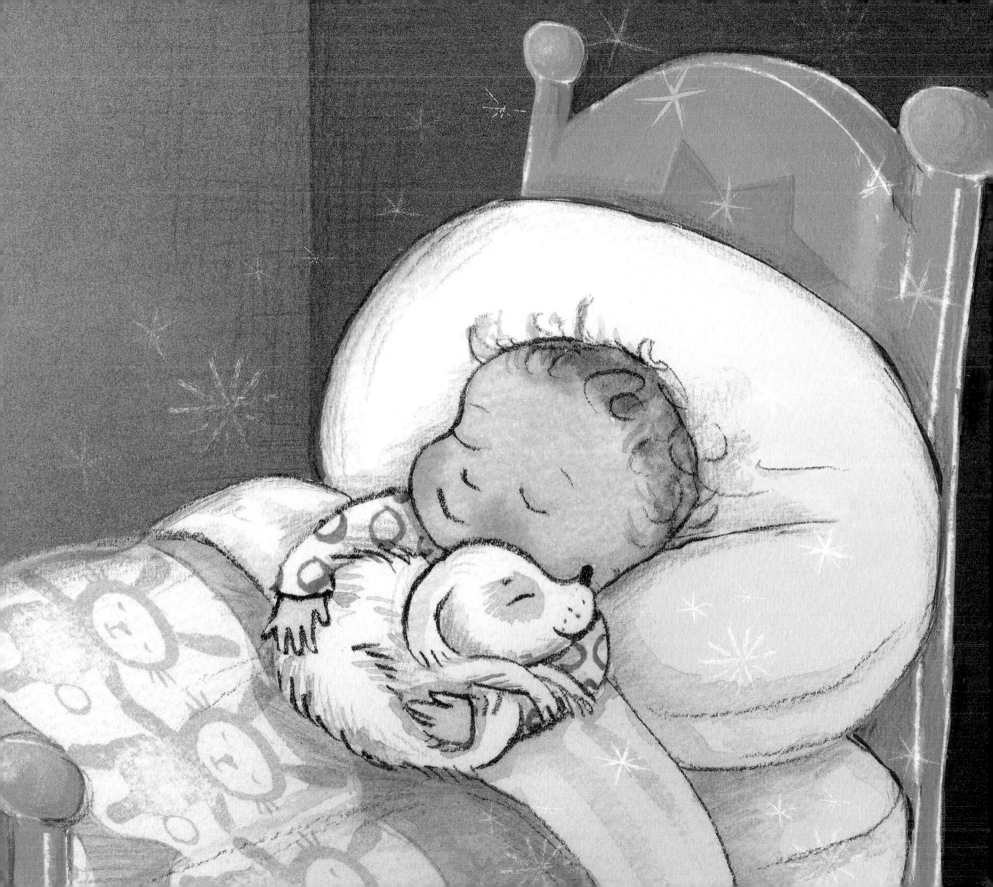

For Sarah K, quiet cheerleader
A. H.

For Maisie Wren Adcock
P. D.

*A special thanks to Charlie Morton who
drew the baby on the bedroom wall.*

First published 2017 by Walker Books Ltd, 87 Vauxhall Walk, London SE11 5HJ
Text © 2017 Amy Hest • Illustrations © 2017 Polly Dunbar • The right of Amy Hest and Polly Dunbar to be identified as
author and illustrator respectively of this work has been asserted by them in accordance with the Copyright, Designs
and Patents Act 1988 • This book has been typeset in HVD Bodedo • Printed in China • All rights reserved. No part of
this book may be reproduced, transmitted or stored in an information retrieval system in any form or by any means,
graphic, electronic or mechanical, including photocopying, taping and recording, without prior written permission
from the publisher. • British Library Cataloguing in Publication Data: a catalogue record for this book is available
from the British Library • ISBN 978-1-4063-7301-1 • www.walker.co.uk • 10 9 8 7 6 5 4 3 2 1

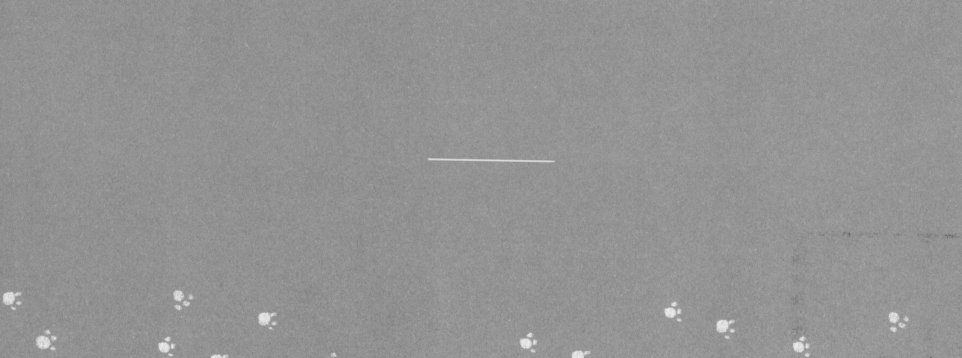